SHERRIN
BEER
EAU DE DAD
HOODOOGURUS

BEER
SHERRIN
EAU DE DAD
HOODOOGURUS

RANDOM HOUSE AUSTRALIA

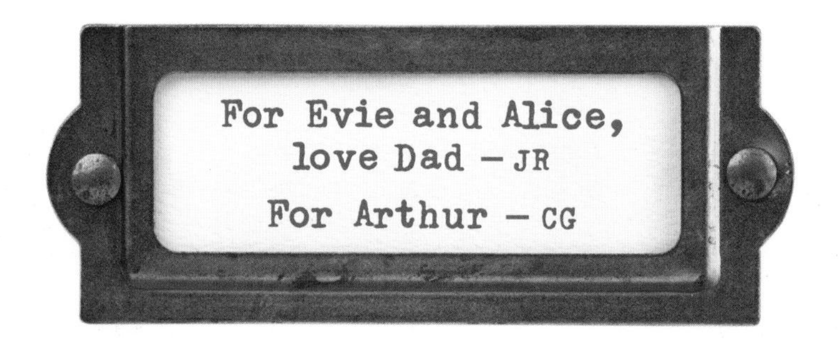

A Random House book
Published by Random House Australia Pty Ltd
Level 3, 100 Pacific Highway, North Sydney NSW 2060
www.randomhouse.com.au

First published by Random House Australia in 2012

Addresses for companies within the Random House Group can be found at www.randomhouse.com.au/offices.

National Library of Australia
Cataloguing-in-Publication Entry

Author: Ractliffe, Justin
Title: Dads: a field guide / Justin Ractliffe; illustrator Cathie Glassby
ISBN: 978 1 74275 549 6 (hbk.)
Dewey number: A823.3

Cover, internal design and typesetting by Cathie Glassby
Printed and bound in China by Midas Printing International Co. Ltd.

The creators would like to thank Julie Burland, Chris Kunz & Emma Moss

DADS

A Field Guide

By Justin Ractliffe
& Cathie Glassby

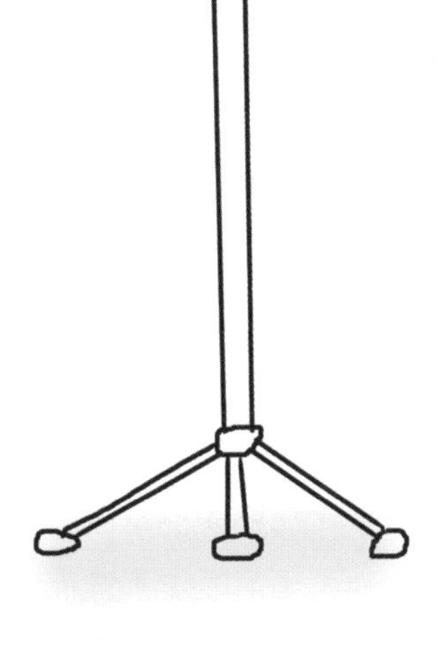

There are all

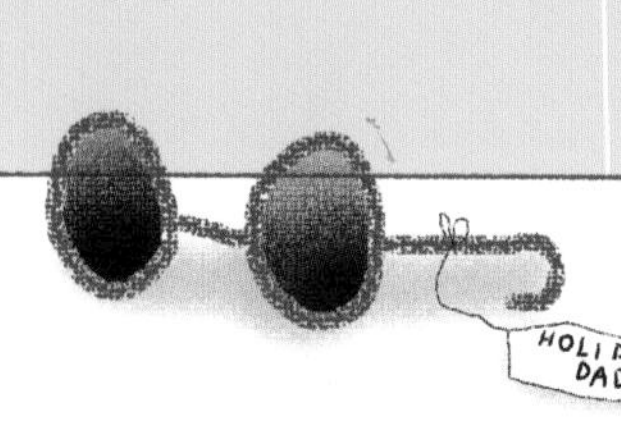

kinds of dads

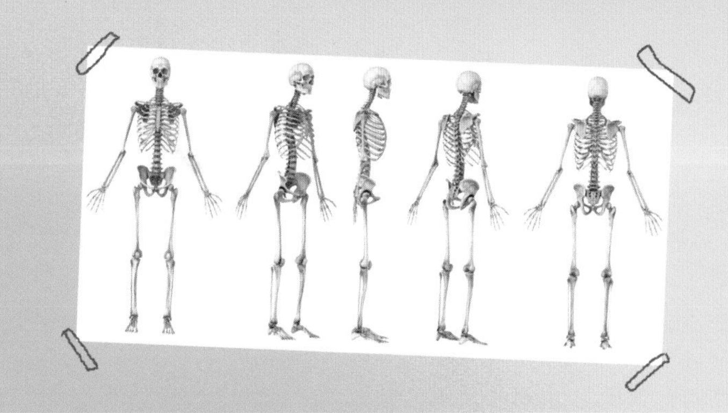

BIG DADS

little dads

Sporty dads

Lazy dads
SHERRIN
BEER
BEER

Boxer dads

Undie dads
HAPPY BIRTHDAY DAD

City dads

Clumsy dads

Car dads

Bike dads

Smart dads

Scruffy dads

Vegie dads

Meaty dads

Surf dads

Golf dads
9

Nerdy dads

Rock 'n' roll dads
THE CRAMPS
STRAY CATS
The CLASH
JD
1
5
10
11
HOODOO GURUS!
AAA

NEW YORK
LONDON
TOKYO
SUCCESS
Work dads
STUFF TO DO
MORE
STUFF TO DO

Holiday dads
50c
Wish you
were
here.
Love
Dad x

Hairy dads

Bald dads

But the best kind of dad is . . .

My dad!